This igloo book belongs to:

....

igloobooks

Written by Marilee Joy Mayfield
Illustrated by Caroline Pedler

Copyright © 2014 Igloo Books Ltd

An imprint of Igloo Books Group,
part of Bonnier Books UK
bonnierbooks.co.uk

Published in 2019
by Igloo Books Ltd, Cottage Farm
Sywell, NN6 0BJ
Manufactured in China. GOL002 0519
10 9 8 7 6 5 4 3 2 1
Library of Congress Cataloging-in-Publication
Data is available upon request.

ISBN 978-1-83852-549-1
IglooBooks.com
bonnierbooks.co.uk

Caroline Pedler   Marilee Joy Mayfield

I Will Always Love You

igloobooks

I will always love you because you're my **family**.
Even though I'm very small, I know you're there for me.

My dad's steps are really huge and mine are baby small.
My dad is big and very strong. He's the best of all.

My mom is kind and gentle. She's very sweet to me.
Even when I mess up, she pretends she doesn't see.

I'm ready for surprises
when Grandpa comes to stay.
Even though he's older,
he remembers how to play!

It's just a simple game
when we're rolling on the ground!

Everything is fun for me
when my brother is around.

My big sister loves to teach me every single day. She shows me things both big and small. I learn as well as play.

I look up to my auntie.

She's fearless, **brave,** and strong.

She makes me feel so safe,

I know nothing can go wrong.

Grandma tells us stories,
the best we've ever heard.
We settle at her feet
and take in every magic word.

I always have such fun when my cousins come to play.
We roll and tumble down the hill...

... playing snowy games all day!

My family is always here
to take good care of me.
When we're snuggled up at night,
we're happy as can be.